STAR WARS®

THE CLONE WARS™

THE BATTLE FOR RYLOTH

Adapted by Zachary Rau

Grosset & Dunlap · LucasBooks

GROSSET & DUNLAP

Published by the Penguin Group

Penguin Group (USA) Inc., 375 Hudson Street, New York, New York 10014, USA

Penguin Group (Canada), 90 Eglinton Avenue East, Suite 700,

Toronto, Ontario M4P 2Y3, Canada

(a division of Pearson Penguin Canada Inc.)

Penguin Books Ltd., 80 Strand, London WC2R 0RL, England

Penguin Group Ireland, 25 St. Stephen's Green, Dublin 2, Ireland

(a division of Penguin Books Ltd.)

Penguin Group (Australia), 250 Camberwell Road, Camberwell, Victoria 3124, Australia

(a division of Pearson Australia Group Pty. Ltd.)

Penguin Books India Pvt. Ltd., 11 Community Centre, Panchsheel Park,

New Delhi—110 017, India

Penguin Group (NZ), 67 Apollo Drive, Rosedale, North Shore 0632, New Zealand

(a division of Pearson New Zealand Ltd.)

Penguin Books (South Africa) (Pty.) Ltd., 24 Sturdee Avenue,

Rosebank, Johannesburg 2196, South Africa

Penguin Books Ltd., Registered Offices:

80 Strand, London WC2R 0RL, England

This book is published in partnership with LucasBooks, a division of Lucasfilm Ltd.

Published by Grosset & Dunlap, a division of Penguin Young Readers Group, 345 Hudson Street, New York, New York 10014. GROSSET & DUNLAP is a trademark of Penguin Group (USA) Inc. Printed in the U.S.A.

Library of Congress Control Number: 2009007020

ISBN 978-0-448-45201-2   10 9 8 7 6 5 4 3 2 1

STORM OVER RYLOTH

Jedi Moral Code #7: It Is A Rough Road That Leads To The Heights Of Greatness.

Subjected to a brutal droid occupation, the people of the planet Ryloth are starving under a blockade by the Separatist Fleet.

The evil Separatist leader, Wat Tambor, now rules with an iron fist. Answering a plea from the senate, the Grand Army of the Republic mounts a bold offensive to liberate the system.

I'M COUNTING ON YOU, CAPTAIN MAR TUUK. WE CANNOT ALLOW THE REPUBLIC TO INVADE THIS PLANET.

It is up to Anakin Skywalker . . .

. . . and his Padawan, Ahsoka Tano, to break the blockade and make way for Obi-Wan's ground assault.

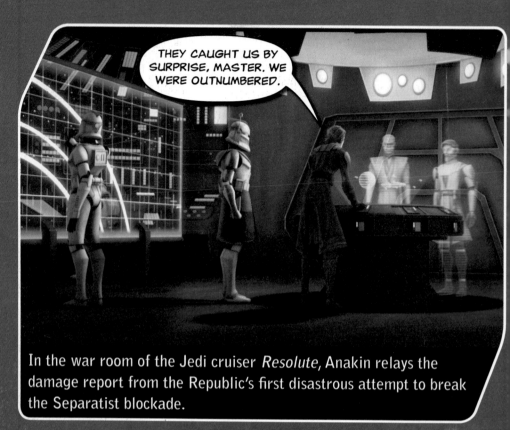

In the war room of the Jedi cruiser *Resolute*, Anakin relays the damage report from the Republic's first disastrous attempt to break the Separatist blockade.

WE LOST A CRUISER, THE *REDEEMER* . . . PLUS AN ENTIRE SQUADRON OF FIGHTERS.

AND YOUR PADAWAN?

AHSOKA IS FINE. LOSING HER SQUADRON WAS HARD TO TAKE.

YOUR FORCES HAVE BEEN CUT IN HALF, SKYWALKER. IF YOU CAN'T BREAK THAT BLOCKADE BEFORE THE NEXT PLANETARY ROTATION, WE WILL HAVE TO POSTPONE THE INVASION.

THE TWI'LEKS ON THAT PLANET CAN'T WAIT FOREVER, MASTER. THE LONGER THE TECHNO UNION KEEPS CONTROL OF RYLOTH, THE MORE DIFFICULT IT WILL BE TO FREE THEM.

I AGREE! WE DON'T HAVE TIME.

As the meeting ends, Anakin must decide what to do next.

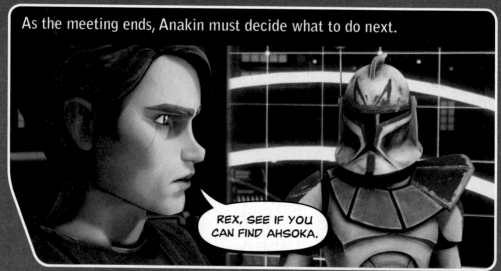

REX, SEE IF YOU CAN FIND AHSOKA.

Later in the hangar . . .

NO ARTOO, THE OTHER ONE.

YOU WANTED TO SEE ME, MASTER?

AHSOKA, HAND ME THAT SOCKET PLUG.

HOW ARE YOU FEELING?

OH . . . I'M FINE, MASTER.

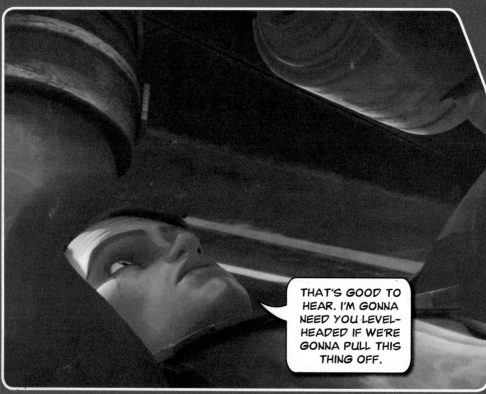

THAT'S GOOD TO HEAR. I'M GONNA NEED YOU LEVEL-HEADED IF WE'RE GONNA PULL THIS THING OFF.

PULL THIS OFF? PULL WHAT OFF, MASTER?!

I TALKED TO MASTER WINDU. WE ARE TO PROCEED WITH OUR ATTACK ON THE BLOCKADE.

WHAT?! MASTER, WE CAN'T! I MEAN, HOW-!

AHSOKA, WE HAVE TO BREAK THAT BLOCKADE. THE TWI'LEKS ON RYLOTH ARE DEPENDING ON US.

I UNDERSTAND THAT, MASTER, BUT WE'VE LOST SO MANY MEN. DID WE GET MORE SUPPORT?

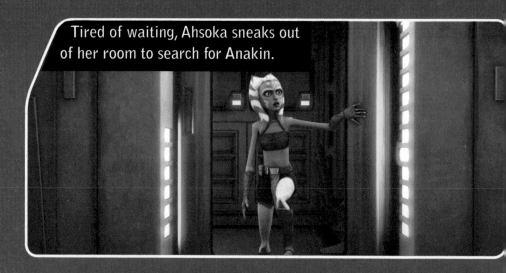

Tired of waiting, Ahsoka sneaks out of her room to search for Anakin.

TROOPER, WHAT'S GOING ON?

THE STARSHIP *DEFENDER* IS BEING EVACUATED, COMMANDER.

EVACUATED? WHY?

NOT SURE, COMMANDER. WE'RE ON OUR WAY TO HELP GENERAL SKYWALKER IN THE HANGAR.

In the hangar . . .

C'MON! MOVE IT! LET'S GO!

MASTER, I'M AFRAID TO ASK.

I ORDERED THE DEFENDER EVACUATED. ACTUALLY, I GOT THE IDEA FROM YOU. YOU SAID WE COULDN'T JUST SMASH THROUGH THE BLOCKADE.

YOU ALSO IMPLIED THAT MY PLANS PUT A LOT OF PEOPLE AT RISK AND I AGREE WITH YOU ON THAT.

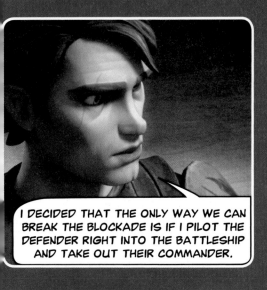

I DECIDED THAT THE ONLY WAY WE CAN BREAK THE BLOCKADE IS IF I PILOT THE DEFENDER RIGHT INTO THE BATTLESHIP AND TAKE OUT THEIR COMMANDER.

THIS WAY I'M THE ONLY ONE AT RISK.

YOU CAN'T BE SERIOUS, MASTER! YOU'LL DIE!

ARTOO AND I WILL GET IN AN ESCAPE POD AND JETTISON RIGHT BEFORE IMPACT.

I'LL BE PRETTY MUCH DEFENSELESS IN AN ESCAPE POD, SO I'M DEPENDING ON YOU TO ENGAGE THE REMAINING FLEET.

THESE MEN ARE DEPENDING ON YOU AND THIS TIME, SO AM I.

TRY TO LEAVE SOME SHIPS FOR US, GENERAL.

WILL DO, REX. COMMANDER AHSOKA WILL FILL YOU IN ON THE FULL PLAN.

Anakin jumps into the shuttle . . .

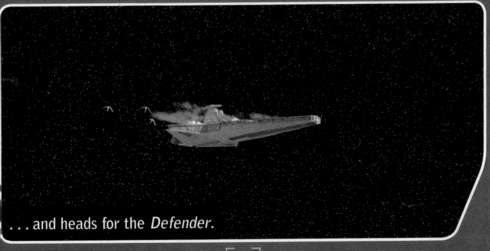

. . . and heads for the *Defender*.

Later in the war room of the *Resolute* . . .

WITH THEIR GENERAL DESTROYED ALONG WITH THEIR BATTLESHIP . . . THE DROID COMMANDERS WILL BE IN CHAOS.

ONLY TEMPORARILY! AND THERE IS STILL GENERAL SKYWALKER TO FIND IN ALL THAT MESS.

EVEN IF SKYWALKER IS SUCCESSFUL AND DESTROYS THE BATTLESHIP, HOW WILL WE STAND UP TO THE COMBINED FIREPOWER OF THE REMAINING FRIGATES?

I THOUGHT ABOUT THAT AND WELL . . . I HAVE AN IDEA.

IF WE TOOK THE RESOLUTE AND ANGLED HER HULL AGAINST THE INCOMING FRIGATES, THE BRIDGE AND HANGAR DECK WOULD BE RELATIVELY SAFE FROM THEIR ATTACK.

WE COULD DRAW THEM IN AND THEN USE THE BOMBERS TO FLANK THEM. THE BOMBERS WOULD BE TOO FAST AND THEY WOULD BE TRAPPED.

Right on schedule,

Anakin flies the *Defender* toward the blockade . . .

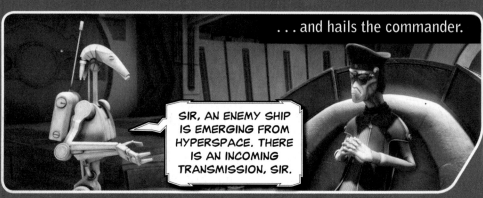

. . . and hails the commander.

SIR, AN ENEMY SHIP IS EMERGING FROM HYPERSPACE. THERE IS AN INCOMING TRANSMISSION, SIR.

GREETINGS, GENERAL! I AM ANAKIN SKYWALKER, GENERAL OF THE GRAND ARMY OF THE REP–

I KNOW WHO YOU ARE, SKYWALKER.

I HAVE BEEN ORDERED TO SURRENDER MYSELF, THE ENTIRE CREW OF THIS VESSEL, AND MY SHIP IN EXCHANGE FOR SAFE PASSAGE OF FOOD AND MEDICAL SUPPLIES TO THE PEOPLE OF RYLOTH.

A NOBLE GESTURE, JEDI. AND YOUR CAPTURE WOULD MAKE ME THE ENVY OF THE SEPARATIST FLEET . . . EVEN GENERAL GRIEVOUS.

WE ARE CLOSING IN. WE'LL PREPARE TO BE BOARDED.

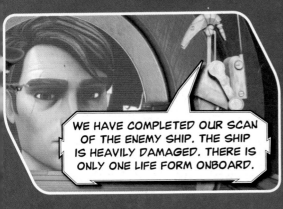

WE HAVE COMPLETED OUR SCAN OF THE ENEMY SHIP. THE SHIP IS HEAVILY DAMAGED. THERE IS ONLY ONE LIFE FORM ONBOARD.

SKYWALKER, WHAT TREACHERY IS THIS?! YOU HAVE NOTHING TO BARGAIN WITH!

IN THAT CASE, I'LL BE GOING! OH, YOU CAN STILL HAVE THE SHIP!

SIR, THERE IS A SECOND REPUBLIC SHIP ENTERING THE SYSTEM.

ALL CANNONS FIRE! FIRE!

IT'S NO USE, SIR! WE CAN'T STOP IT. WHAT SHOULD WE DO?

WE DIE!!!

The *Defender* plows right into the bridge of the command ship . . .

. . . setting off a chain of explosions that destroys the entire ship.

SEE, I TOLD YOU IT WOULD WORK.

Anakin watches the fireworks from the safety of an escape pod.

On one of the remaining Separatist blockade vessels . . .

THE GENERAL WENT DOWN WITH HIS SHIP. WHAT SHOULD WE DO?

WHO'S IN CHARGE?

NOT ME!

NOT ME!

NOT ME!

OKAY, HOLD YOUR POSITIONS.

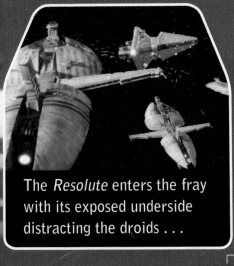

The *Resolute* enters the fray with its exposed underside distracting the droids . . .

BOOM!

KZZZZH!

... while Ahsoka leads a squad of bombers around the outside flank of the blockade.

OKAY, BOYS! HERE WE GO! FOLLOW MY LEAD!

The bombers strafe the Separatist frigates with laser fire, dropping bombs on each run.

ZAAAKT!

KZZZKST!

BOOM!

I KNOW THAT STRATEGY. THAT A GIRL, AHSOKA.

As Anakin watches the destruction from his escape pod, he drifts further away from the battle.

WE'VE BEEN OUTFLANKED!

BOOM

AHHHH-KSSSSH!

BOOM

AFFIRMATIVE!

One by one the other frigates are destroyed by Republic fire ...

... until the blockade is nothing more than a collection of battered ships.

AHSOKA, THIS IS OBI-WAN.

CAN WE BEGIN OUR LANDING?

YES, MASTER! YOU ARE CLEARED FOR GROUND ASSAULT!

I WON'T EVEN ASK WHERE THE REST OF ANAKIN'S FLEET IS OR WHY HE'S IN AN ESCAPE POD.

THAT'S PROBABLY FOR THE BEST.

THE INNOCENTS OF RYLOTH

Jedi Moral Code #8: The Costs Of War
Can Never Be Truly Accounted For.

On the surface of the planet Ryloth . . .

Invasion! Jedi Generals Mace Windu and Obi-Wan Kenobi lead a massive invasion to liberate the starving people.

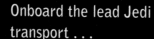

Onboard the lead Jedi transport . . .

WE'RE GOING TO HAVE TO TAKE THIS PLANET ONE CITY AT A TIME.

THE FIRST TRICK WILL BE GETTING OUR TROOPS ON THE GROUND.

IF YOU TAKE THE CITY OF NABAT FIRST, WE'LL HAVE OUR LANDING ZONE.

WELL, IT'S TIME TO MEET THE NATIVES.

THE INVASION MUST BE STOPPED IN THE AIR. YOU MUST NOT ALLOW THE CLONES TO REACH THE SURFACE.

OUR NEW PROTON CANNONS ARE IN THE OPTIMUM POSITION TO PREVENT THAT, SIR.

WHAT IF THEY FOCUS THE ATTACK ON THE CANNONS?

I AM UTILIZING THE PRISONERS FROM THIS VILLAGE AS LIVING SHIELDS.

I CALCULATE THE JEDI WILL NOT RISK THEIR SAFETY WITH A DIRECT ASSAULT.

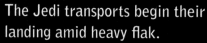
The Jedi transports begin their landing amid heavy flak.

WE NEED TO REMEMBER WHY WE'RE HERE. WE CAME TO AID THE TWI'LEKS NOT DESTROY THEIR HOME.

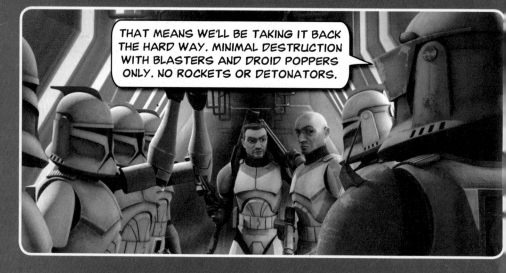
THAT MEANS WE'LL BE TAKING IT BACK THE HARD WAY. MINIMAL DESTRUCTION WITH BLASTERS AND DROID POPPERS ONLY. NO ROCKETS OR DETONATORS.

CHECK YOUR AIM. KEEP AN EYE OUT FOR THE LOCALS. AM I UNDERSTOOD?

SIR, YES SIR!

SIR, YES SIR!

SIR, YES SIR!

The closer the ships get to the city, the heavier the flak gets.

BOOM!

GET ME KENOBI!

GENERAL, THE ENEMY FIRE IS PENETRATING OUR SHIELDS!

WE CAN'T RISK LANDING THE LARGER TRANSPORTS . . .

. . . UNTIL YOU TAKE OUT THOSE GUNS.

PULL BACK. WE'LL TAKE CARE OF IT.

WHO'S UP FOR A CHALLENGE? WE'RE NOT GETTING ANY REINFORCEMENTS UNTIL THOSE GUNS ARE OUT OF COMMISSION.

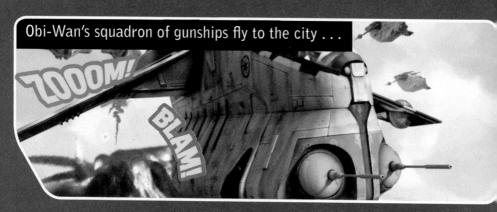

Obi-Wan's squadron of gunships fly to the city . . .

ZOOOM!

BLAM!

. . . but just out of range of the guns.

PAM!
PAM!
POM!

COMMANDER, THE REPUBLIC TRANSPORTS HAVE TURNED AWAY, BUT THE GUNSHIPS ARE STILL HEADING TOWARD US.

JUST AS I CALCULATED.

PREPARE FOR THEIR GROUND ASSAULT.

The gunships touch down a few clicks outside the city . . .

GO! GO!

WHOOSH!

COME ON, MEN!

THAT BUNKER IS GOING TO BE A PROBLEM, GENERAL.

LEAVE THE BUNKER TO ME! BRING IN YOUR TROOPERS ON MY SIGNAL!

YOU TWO WANTED ACTION? FOLLOW ME!

One of the clones, Boil, throws an EMP grenade into the crow's nest . . .

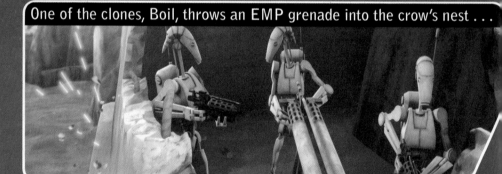

. . . that knocks out the droid's electrical systems.

THE WALL IS SECURE, SIR. ARE WE MOVING ON TO THE GUNS?!

WE NEED TO KNOW WHAT THE DROIDS HAVE IN STORE FOR US. SEND YOUR BEST MEN TO SCOUT AHEAD.

BOIL! WAXER! COME WITH ME!

BUILDINGS ARE JUST BUILDINGS. WHAT REALLY MAKES A CITY IS THE PEOPLE WHO LIVE IN IT.

SO WHERE ARE THEY?

Elsewhere in the city . . .

NOT GONNA BE EASY GETTING TO THOSE GUNS, SIR.

THERE'S ALWAYS A WAY.

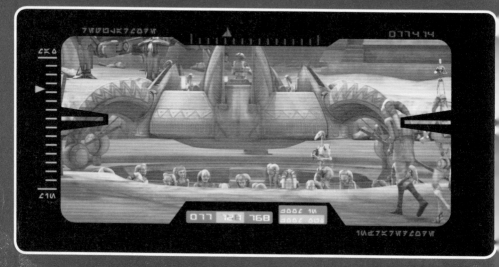

WAIT! TWI'LEKS! THEY'RE HOLDING ALL OF THE SURVIVORS HOSTAGE.

WE HAVE TO REPORT THIS TO GENERAL KENOBI.

Later . . .

WE FOUND THE GUNS. THEY'RE IN THE COURTYARD HERE AND HERE, BUT THERE'S A COMPLICATION.

THEY'VE TAKEN THE LOCALS HOSTAGE AND THEY'RE USING THEM AS SHIELDS.

THE TWI'LEK PRISONERS WILL MAKE THIS DIFFICULT, BUT NOT IMPOSSIBLE.

I STILL HAVE A GOOD PLAN FOR TAKING OUT THOSE GUNS.

GETTING THE VILLAGERS OUT OF HARM'S WAY IS OUR FIRST PRIORITY! I HAVE FAITH IN YOU, GENERAL KENOBI.

CODY, WE'LL GO IN WITH EVERYTHING WE HAVE. CLEAR THOSE HOSTAGES.

IT'S JUST A LITTLE GIRL.

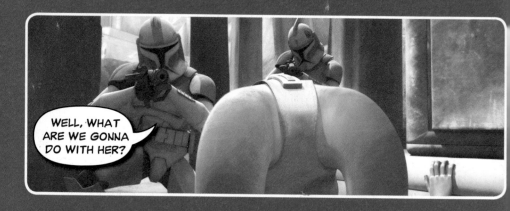

WELL, WHAT ARE WE GONNA DO WITH HER?

WHY DO WE HAVE TO DO ANYTHING? WE'VE GOT A MISSION TO FINISH.

WE SHOULD DO SOMETHING. I SAY WE TAKE HER WITH US.

YOU CAN'T BE SERIOUS! SHE'LL ONLY SLOW US DOWN.

WE CAN'T LEAVE HER HERE.

FINE! WE TAKE HER.

COME HERE, YOU!

STOP! YOU'RE SCARING HER. SHE PROBABLY THINKS WE'RE DROIDS.

IT'S ALL RIGHT! SEE? I'M FLESH AND BLOOD . . . JUST LIKE YOU.

SHE LOOKS HALF STARVED.

HERE.

NERRA, NERRA . . .

CHOMP! CHOMP!

YOU MADE A FRIEND, MISSION ACCOMPLISHED. CAN WE GO NOW?!

COME ON, KID. COME ON.

LOOK, SHE DOESN'T EVEN WANT TO GO. THE LITTLE MONSTER WAS FINE BEFORE WE CAME ALONG, SO LET'S MOVE.

SERGEANT, ARE THE CREATURES READY?!

I STARVED THEM LIKE YOU ORDERED, SIR. ARE YOU SURE THEY WILL NOT ATTACK US?

I NEED A TEST TO VERIFY MY THEORY.

CLICK!

TX-20 pushes the cage release button . . .

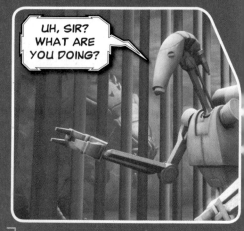

UH, SIR? WHAT ARE YOU DOING?

SERGEANT, THEY ARE PREPARING TO ATTACK. RELEASE THE BEASTS. IT IS TIME TO EXECUTE MY PLAN.

The droids release the starving Gutkurr beasts . . .

ROGER, ROGER!

. . . and usher them up into the city.

The Gutkurr charge through the streets, searching for something to eat.

The Gutkurr easily sniff out the clone troopers.

THE REPUBLIC TROOPS HAVE BEEN ROUTED, EMIR.

BOOM!

WHAT WAS THAT?

I CALCULATE THE REMAINING CLONES ARE ATTEMPTING A DESPERATE FINAL OFFENSIVE. THEIR CHANCES ARE 742 TO 1.

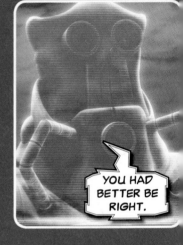

YOU HAD BETTER BE RIGHT.

I AM A DROID. I AM ALWAYS RIGHT.

On the other side of the city . . .

Obi-Wan stands directly in the path of the beasts . . .

. . . and uses the Force to influence the simpleminded creatures.

Obi-Wan leads the creatures down a narrow dead end.

SHOOT THE BRIDGE!

The clones aim for a rock bridge overhead.

KAZZAK!

CRACK!
BOOM!

The bridge shatters under the barrage of laser fire and falls to the ground, trapping the beasts and Obi-Wan.

Obi-Wan jumps over the beasts . . .

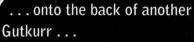

. . . onto the back of another Gutkurr . . .

. . . and past the rock barricade.

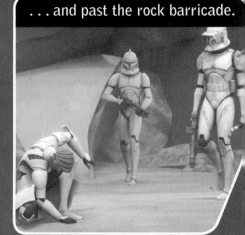

Suddenly, a manhole cover spooks the clones . . .

. . . but Obi-Wan senses the presence of clones.

DON'T SHOOT!

WAXER, BOIL, WHERE HAVE YOU BEEN?!

SIR, THERE'S AN EXPLANATION.

WE GOT SIDETRACKED.

I THINK I SEE WHAT SIDETRACKED YOU.

HELLO, LITTLE ONE.

SHE BROUGHT US HERE THROUGH THE TUNNELS. KNOWS HER WAY AROUND THEM PRETTY GOOD, SIR.

OOH YANA-YANA. WAH NERRA. KUMEE NERRA.

THE GIRL CAN LEAD US THROUGH THE TUNNEL TO THE PRISONERS.

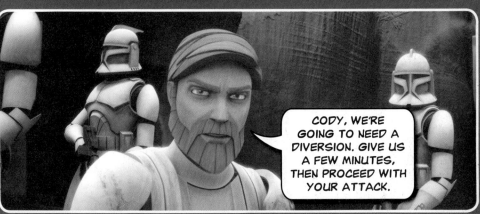

CODY, WE'RE GOING TO NEED A DIVERSION. GIVE US A FEW MINUTES, THEN PROCEED WITH YOUR ATTACK.

YOU GOT IT, SIR!

Shortly, in the tunnels . . .

UH OH!

I'LL TAKE CARE OF THIS. YOU KEEP HER HERE.

Obi-Wan sneaks out into the town square.

HMMM?

On the other side of the square, the clone army creates a diversion.

The easily distracted droid army engages the clones . . .

. . . leaving the Twi'lek prisoners sparsely guarded.

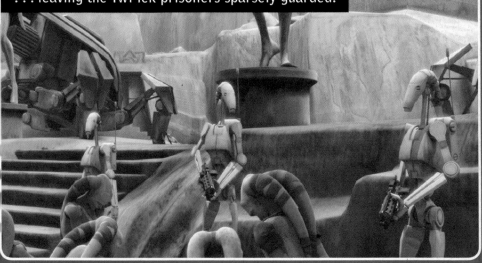

Obi-Wan and the rest of the clones sneak up behind the remaining droids . . .

. . . and easily dispatch them.

Obi-Wan frees the Twi'leks . . .

. . . and leads them into the safety of the underground tunnels.

NUMA! KOMA JEL REE-KHA!

HA-HA-HA-HA-HA!

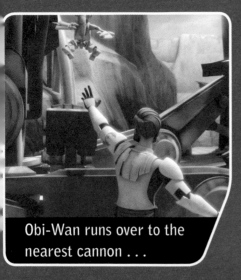

Obi-Wan runs over to the nearest cannon . . .

. . . while the clones load it.

Obi-Wan destroys the remaining cannons.

KA-BOOM!

Focused on the destruction of the other cannons, Obi-Wan fails to sense a flanking Separatist tank.

The tank fires on the cannon . . .

RUN!

BLAZZZKT!

BOOM!

. . . destroying it.

NERRA?

The Twi'lek girl rushes to Obi-Wan as the tank rumbles toward the Jedi.

With one of their offspring in danger, the Twi'lek people decide to take matters into their own hands.

YARRRGH!

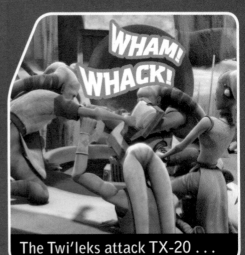

WHAM!
WHACK!

The Twi'leks attack TX-20 . . .

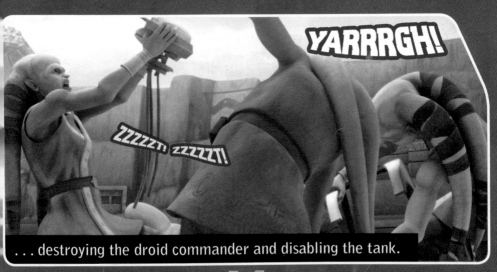

YARRRGH!

ZZZZZT! ZZZZZT!

. . . destroying the droid commander and disabling the tank.

With the cannons destroyed, the rest of the Republic army is able to land.

GREAT JOB GETTING RID OF THOSE CANNONS.

NOW WE HAVE TO TAKE THE CAPITAL AND FREE THIS WORLD.

SEE YA LATER, LITTLE ONE.

HEY, STAY OUT OF TROUBLE.

LIBERTY ON RYLOTH

Republic victory is at hand! Clone troopers under the command of the Jedi have successfully invaded the Separatist occupied world of Ryloth.

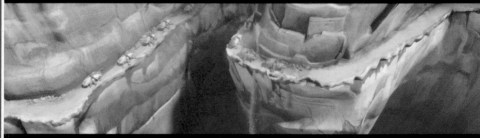

Now, Jedi General Mace Windu leads the attack on enemy lines in the final offensive to liberate the capital city of Lessu.

Mace Windu leads a convoy of Republic walkers along a wide ravine . . .

FIRE!

. . . when Separatist forces ambush them.

The lead walker takes a direct hit and is disabled.

TAKE COVER!

Commander Ponds uses his wrist radio to communicate with the platoon.

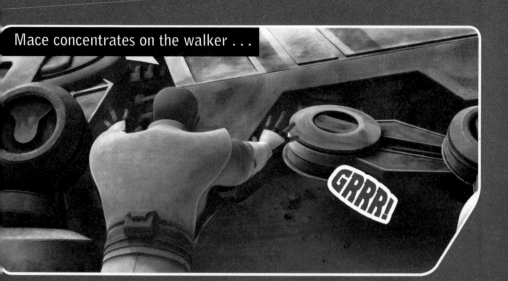

Mace concentrates on the walker . . .

GRRR!

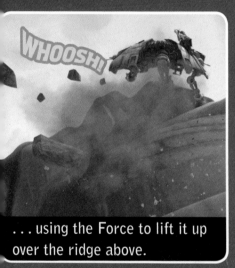

WHOOSH!

. . . using the Force to lift it up over the ridge above.

FIND SOME COVER! MOVE IT! LET'S GO!

WE'LL LEAD THE WAY, COMMANDER!

Mace jumps onto a two-legged AT-RT walker . . .

SIR, THE ENEMY IS ADVANCING AGAIN.

NOW THAT JEDI IS LEADING THE ATTACK IN SMALLER WALKERS, ORDER OUR GUNNERS TO BLAST THEM!

Mace and a squad of troopers on AT-RTs head straight for the Separatist tanks.

THE JEDI IS STILL COMING!

FIRE EVERYTHING WE'VE GOT . . . NOW!

BOOM!

BOOM!

BOOM!

Suddenly, Mace and the other clones are right on top of the droids . . .

. . . and quickly destroy the tank unit.

Mace talks freely about the Republic's plans to take over the capital, not realizing that the entire conversation is being overheard.

GENERAL WINDU HAS BROKEN OUR LINES?! THE REPUBLIC IS ADVANCING FASTER THAN I EXPECTED.

I CALCULATE THEY WILL REACH THE MAIN GATES BY MORNING. I RECOMMEND WE PREPARE OUR RETREAT.

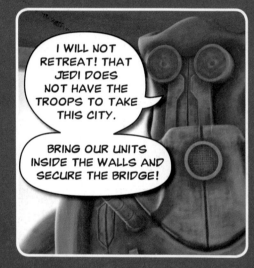

I WILL NOT RETREAT! THAT JEDI DOES NOT HAVE THE TROOPS TO TAKE THIS CITY.

BRING OUR UNITS INSIDE THE WALLS AND SECURE THE BRIDGE!

WHAT ABOUT THE CITY INHABITANTS?

DRIVE THEM OUTSIDE, BUT NOT TOO FAR. THE JEDI WILL RECONSIDER AN ATTACK WHEN HE SEES THEM IN HIS LINE OF FIRE.

The convoy of walkers pushes toward the capital.

Inside the lead walker, Mace meets with the Jedi Council.

WHAT'S YOUR PROGRESS, SKYWALKER?

MY FIGHTERS HAVE SECURED CONTROL OF THE SPACE AROUND RYLOTH. WE HAVE THE SEPARATIST CRUISERS ON THE RUN.

MASTER KENOBI HAS TAKEN THE JIXUAN DESERT, SO THE SOUTHERN HEMISPHERE IS OURS.

THEN IT'S ALMOST OVER.

NOT YET. THE FINAL KEY POSITION IS THE CAPITAL OF LESSU. OUR SPIES ARE CERTAIN WAT TAMBOR HAS HIS COMMAND CENTER THERE.

WHEN TAKEN THE CITY WE HAVE . . . CAPTURE TAMBOR, WE MUST!

IT'S NOT GOING TO BE EASY, MASTER. TAMBOR HAS CHOSEN HIS STRONGHOLD WELL.

THIS PLASMA BRIDGE IS THE ONLY WAY IN OR OUT.

I'M AFRAID A SIEGE COULD DRAG ON INDEFINITELY.

MY PEOPLE HAVE ALREADY SUFFERED SO MUCH.

WITH OUR FORCES STRETCHED SO THINLY, I'M GOING TO ENLIST THE HELP OF THE FREEDOM FIGHTERS LED BY CHAM SYNDULLA.

HIS FIGHT AGAINST THE DROIDS HAS MADE HIM A SYMBOL OF FREEDOM FOR THE PEOPLE.

CHAM SYNDULLA WAS A RADICAL BEFORE THE WAR. HE IS VERY UNPREDICTABLE.

HE CAN'T BE TRUSTED. I KNOW SYNDULLA SEEKS TO GAIN POWER. WE WERE POLITICAL RIVALS.

I'LL LEAVE THE POLITICS TO YOU, SENATOR. I'M DOING WHATEVER I CAN TO HELP THESE PEOPLE.

PERHAPS WE CAN SEND YOU REPUBLIC REINFORCEMENTS INSTEAD.

THERE ARE NO REINFORCEMENTS.

WE CAN'T WIN WITHOUT SYNDULLA'S HELP.

YOUR TACTICAL DROID HAS INFORMED ME OF THE PITIFUL JOB YOU HAVE DONE PROTECTING OUR INVESTMENT ON RYLOTH.

THE DROID EXAGGERATES! I HAVE NOT LOST YET.

YOU ARE NO MATCH FOR MASTER WINDU. DO NOT GET GREEDY, EMIR TAMBOR. TAKE WHAT VALUABLES YOU CAN AND DESTROY EVERYTHING ELSE.

EVERYTHING?

WE CAN PUT THIS DEFEAT TO POLITICAL USE. THE CHARRED RUINS OF RYLOTH WILL DEMONSTRATE TO THE GALAXY THE COST OF A REPUBLIC VICTORY.

DID YOU HEAR THAT?

I DON'T SEE ANYTHING!

WHY DIDN'T WE TAKE 'EM OUT, SIR?

I HAVE A FEELING SOMEONE ELSE WILL DO IT FOR US.

BAM!!

BLAM!!

LOOK OUT!

IT'S AN AMBUSH!

BOOM!

Hearing the sounds of battle, Mace immediately jumps to attention
. . . ready for a fight.

I WAS WONDERING
WHEN YOU'D FIND
ME, MASTER JEDI.

I'VE COME FOR
YOUR HELP,
GENERAL
SYNDULLA.

WHAT MAKES
YOU THINK
YOU'LL GET IT?

The Lessu Palace . . .

EMIR TAMBOR, OUR BOMBERS ARE NEARLY READY FOR LAUNCH.

TARGET EVERY TWI'LEK VILLAGE IN RANGE—THE INHABITED ONES FIRST.

OF COURSE, THEN I WILL READY YOUR SHIP FOR EVACUATION.

NO, I AM NOT YET READY TO LEAVE.

That night . . .

HAVE OUR SCOUTS REPORTED IN FROM THE VILLAGE UP AHEAD?

THE ENEMY HAS PULLED OUT, SIR.

FRIENDLIES ARE ALL THAT'S LEFT. MOSTLY WOMEN AND CHILDREN.

SEE IF WE CAN SPARE SOME RATIONS. THEY'LL BE HUNGRY.

SIR, ENEMY SHIPS ARE ENTERING OUR SECTOR.

DAMAGE REPORT!

THERE'S NO TACTICAL DAMAGE, SIR. THEY DIDN'T HIT US . . .

THEY BOMBED THE VILLAGE!

MAKE CONTACT WITH GENERAL WINDU.

Inside Cham Syndulla's secret hideout . . .

I HOPE YOU DON'T MIND THIS. A LITTLE DISTRACTION GOES FAR TO EASE THE BURDEN OF THE WAR ON MY MEN.

YOU HAVE PROVIDED WELL FOR YOUR MEN. ALL YOUR PEOPLE. SO WHY WON'T YOU HELP ME FREE THEM FROM THIS OCCUPATION?

I DON'T TRUST SENATOR TAA . . . HIS PLANS FOR OUR WORLD AFTER THE WAR.

THE REPUBLIC WILL HELP YOU REBUILD. WE WON'T ABANDON YOU.

ANOTHER ARMED
OCCUPATION IS NOT
A FREE RYLOTH!
HOW LONG BEFORE
I AM FIGHTING YOU,
MASTER JEDI?

Mace's wrist-communicator
interrupts their conversation.

BEEP!
BEEP!
BEEP!

WHAT IS IT,
COMMANDER?

THE DROIDS HAVE BEGUN
A FIREBOMBING CAMPAIGN.
SEVERAL VILLAGES IN
OUR SECTOR HAVE BEEN
DESTROYED.

MAKE THE
ARRANGEMENTS . . .
I WILL SPEAK TO
SENATOR TAA.

Shortly . . .

SENATOR TAA, SO GLAD YOU COULD JOIN US FROM COMFORTABLE CORUSCANT!

NEED I REMIND YOU THAT IT IS I WHO LEADS OUR PEOPLE IN THE SENATE!

AND IT IS I WHO LEADS OUR PEOPLE HERE AND NOW!

THERE WILL BE NOTHING LEFT TO LEAD IF YOU REFUSE TO WORK TOGETHER.

I HEAR YOU, SKYWALKER.

GENERAL WINDU, DO YOU COPY?

MY FIGHTERS ARE TAKING OUT ALL THE BOMBERS AS FAST AS THEY CAN, MASTER WINDU, BUT THERE ARE JUST TOO MANY.

I DOUBT WE CAN STOP THEM ALL. I SUGGEST YOU GET THE PEOPLE AWAY FROM THE CITIES.

ALL RIGHT, DO THE BEST THAT YOU CAN, SKYWALKER.

SENATOR, YOUR PEOPLE ARE HESITANT TO JOIN US BECAUSE THEY'RE WORRIED THERE WILL BE ANOTHER MILITARY OCCUPATION.

MY PEOPLE HAVE OUR PROMISE THAT THE CLONE ARMY WILL LEAVE ONCE RYLOTH IS FREE OF THOSE DROIDS.

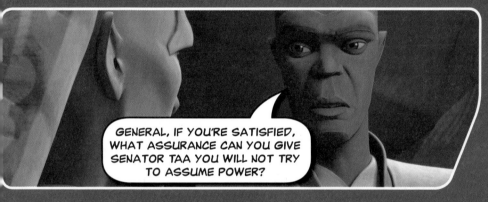

GENERAL, IF YOU'RE SATISFIED, WHAT ASSURANCE CAN YOU GIVE SENATOR TAA YOU WILL NOT TRY TO ASSUME POWER?

I ONLY WANT TO SEE MY PEOPLE FREE, MASTER JEDI. I GIVE MY WORD. I BELIEVE IN DEMOCRACY!

THEN WE ARE TOGETHER IN THIS.

The next day at sun up . . .

TAMBOR IS STILL THERE.

HOW ARE WE GOING TO ATTACK WITH MY PEOPLE SO CLOSE?

YOUR PEOPLE WILL NEVER BE IN DANGER IF OUR WALKERS CAN CROSS THE BRIDGE INTO THE CITY. GETTING CONTROL OF THE BRIDGE IS THE KEY.

PERHAPS THERE IS A WAY.

MY SPIES TELL ME THOSE TRANSPORTS CARRY TREASURE.

YOU THINK WE CAN USE THEM TO GET ACROSS THE BRIDGE?

IT IS RISKY. THEY ARE USUALLY SCANNED WHILE CROSSING.

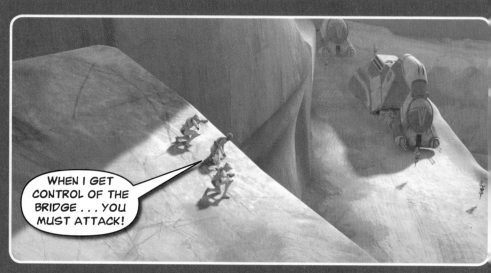

WHEN I GET CONTROL OF THE BRIDGE . . . YOU MUST ATTACK!

VSSSSSSH!

THEY'RE IN! LET'S GO!

As the transports arrive, two droids activate the laser bridge to the city.

ALL RIGHT, HOLD IT THERE! LET'S GET THESE TRANSPORTS SCANNED.

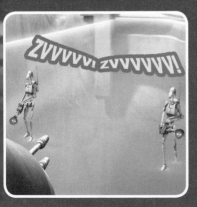

ZVVVVV! ZVVVVVV!

HERE THEY COME!

I'M PICKING UP AN ANOMALY IN THERE.

WE BETTER CHECK IT OUT. OPEN THE CARGO HATCH!

The second the hatch opens, Mace and the clones attack the droids guarding the gate.

OH NO! IT'S A JEDI!

RUN FOR IT! THEY'RE TURNING THE BRIDGE OFF!

As the bridge disappears, Mace jumps . . .

. . . and barely grabs hold of the ledge.

I'LL HOLD THEM OFF! GET THAT BRIDGE BACK UP!!

SIR, YES SIR!

The clones blast their way to the control tower . . .

. . . and activate the bridge.

Cham Syndulla's freedom fighters and a squadron of clones pour across the bridge to reinforce the Jedi.

CHARGE!

Mace Windu continues to push toward the center of the city, single-handedly taking out a full regiment of droids.

VZZZZZZH!

SMASH!

BOOM!

YOU TAKE THESE DROIDS! I'M GONNA FIND WAT TAMBOR!

All throughout the city the battle rages.

The Republic fighters quickly gain the advantage and send the droid army retreating deeper into the city.

Not far away in the center of the city, TA-175 decides this is the right time to make his escape.

He takes off just as Wat Tambor heads toward his ship.

MY SHIP!

Onboard the ship, TA-175 contacts Count Dooku . . .

I'M AFRAID EMIR TAMBOR REFUSED TO RETREAT IN TIME.

THAT IS UNFORTUNATE. ORDER OUR BOMBERS TO DESTROY THE CAPITAL IMMEDIATELY!

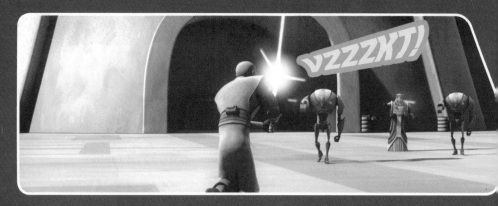

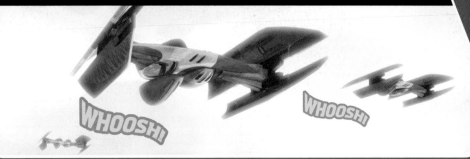

Suddenly . . .

WHOA! THAT WAS CLOSE, MASTER!

ISN'T IT ALWAYS, SNIPS?

The End.

AVAILABLE NOW!

On a secret mission to forge a treaty with King Katuunko of the strategic system of Toydaria, Jedi Master Yoda is ambushed by the sinister Count Dooku. Now, the diminutive Jedi Master and three clone troopers are forced to face off against Dooku's dreaded assassin Asajj Ventress and her massive droid army. Will the Force protect them, or will the dark side finally prevail?